Little Princess

THIS BOOK BELONGS TO

_____

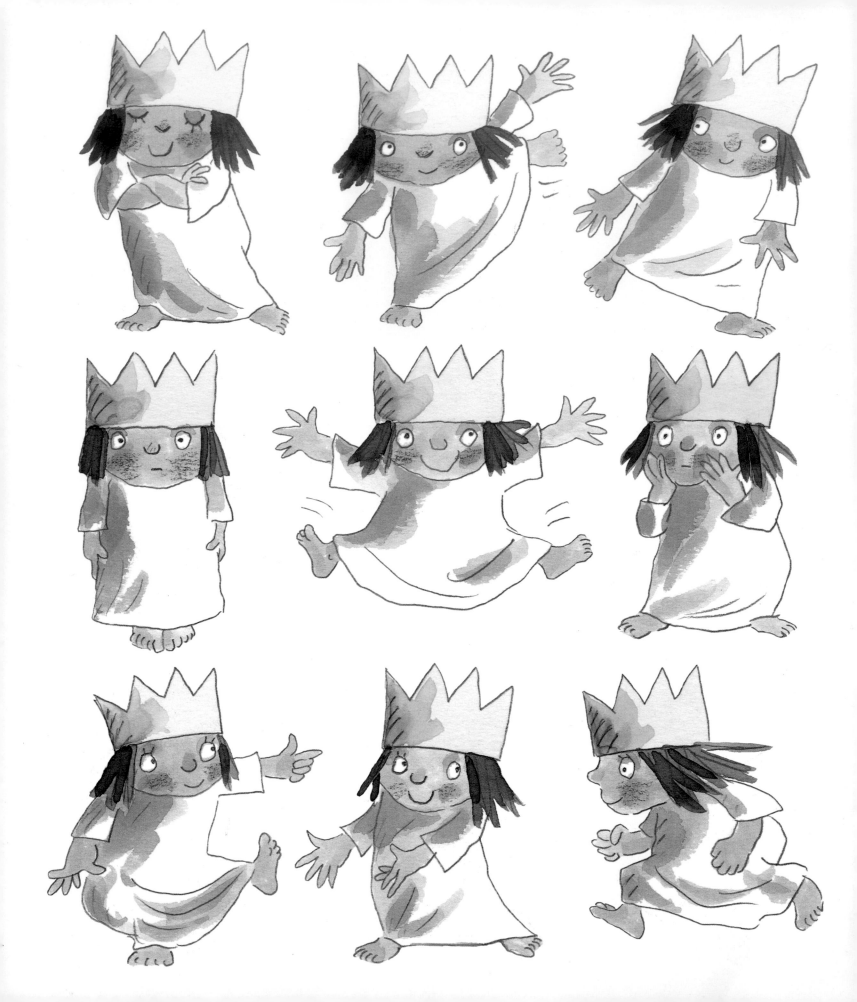

This paperback edition first published in 2017 by Andersen Press Ltd.
First published in Great Britain in 2001 by Andersen Press Ltd.,
20 Vauxhall Bridge Road, London SW1V 2SA
Text and Illustration copyright © Tony Ross, 2001
The rights of Tony Ross to be identified as the author and illustrator of this work have
been asserted by him in accordance with the Copyright, Designs and Patents Act, 1988.
All rights reserved.
Colour separated in Switzerland by Photolitho AG, Zürich.
Printed and bound in Malaysia

1   3   5   7   9   10   8   6   4   2

British Library Cataloguing in Publication Data available.
ISBN 978 1 78344 579 0

Little Princess

I Don't Want to Wash My Hands!

Tony Ross

Andersen Press

"Wheeeeeeeeeee!"
The Little Princess LOVED getting dirty.

"Wash your hands before you eat that," said the Queen.
"Why?" said the Little Princess.

"Because you've been playing outside,"
said the Queen.

"Wash your hands," said the Cook.
"Why?" said the Little Princess.

"Because you've been playing with Scruff.
And dry them properly."

"Wash your hands," said the King.
"Why? I've washed them TWICE,"
said the Little Princess.

"And you must wash them again
because you've just been on your potty."

"Wash your hands," said the Maid.

"I washed them after playing outside.
I washed them after playing with the dog.
I washed them after going on my potty.
I washed them after sneezing...

... WHY?" said the Little Princess.
"Because of germs and nasties," said the Maid.
"What are germs and nasties?" said the Little Princess.

"They're HORRIBLE!" said the Maid.

"They live in the dirties...

... and on the animals...

... and in the sneezes.

Then they can get into your food,
and then into your tummy...

... and then they make you ill."

"What do germs and nasties look like?" said the Little Princess.
"Worse than crocodiles," said the Maid.

"I've got no crocodiles on MY hands."

"Germs and nasties are smaller than crocodiles,"
said the Maid. "They are too small to see."

"I'd better wash my hands again," said the Little Princess.

"Do I have to wash my hands after washing my hands?"

"Don't be silly," said the Maid. "Eat your cake."

"Have you washed YOUR hands?"

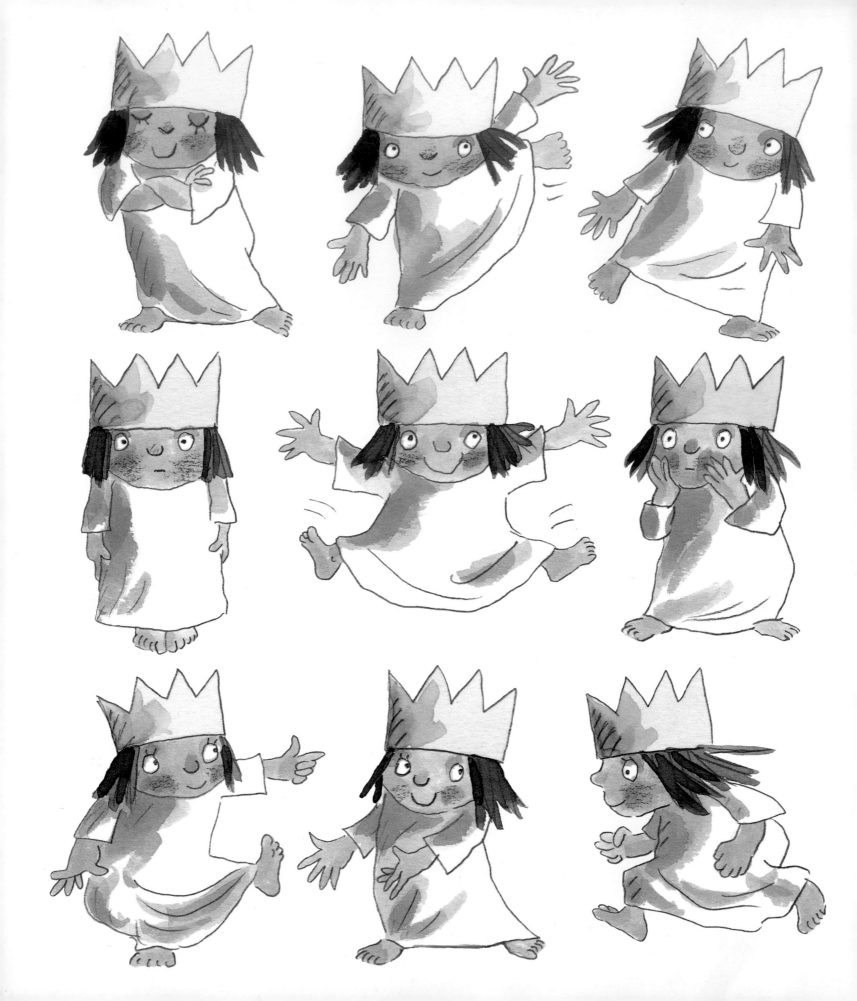